Creative Director: Susie Garland Rice

10754 a/The Silly Swamp of Shapes

The Silly Swamp of Shapes

Dalmatian Press

Written and Illustrated by
Wes Ware

Welcome to the swamp of shapes—
it's the place to be.
Let's make sure we have some fun
with every shape we see.

The creatures in this silly swamp
will help along the way.
They love to play with all these shapes
each and every day.

Harvey Hippo had a circle.
On top of it he sat.
His circle is an **oval** now.
He almost squashed it flat.

There's three more shapes for you to see.
A **heart** is one of them.
It's given by Samantha Snake
to Salamander Sam.

A **star** can have a lot of points;
this one has just five.
Harry Hornet wears a **star**.
He's the sheriff of the hive.

Diamond

When angelfish swim tail to tail
a **diamond**'s what you see.
Hold your finger to the page
and trace the shape with me.

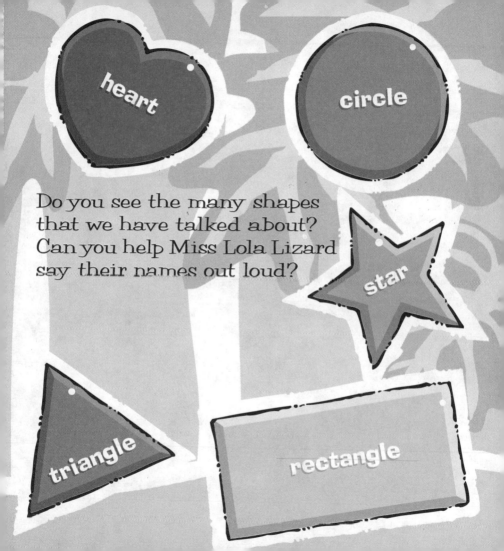

heart

circle

Do you see the many shapes
that we have talked about?
Can you help Miss Lola Lizard
say their names out loud?

star

triangle

rectangle

We've seen a lot of shapes today
in this, our little book.
Come back soon, we'll start again
and have another look.

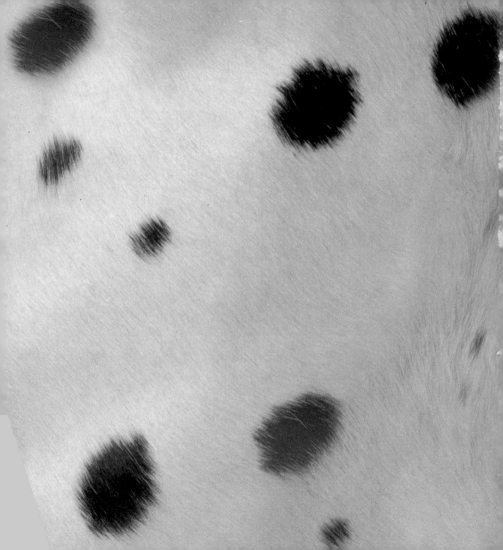